Adapted by Mary Tillworth
Based on the original screenplay by Elise Allen
Illustrated by Ulkutay Design Group

Special thanks to Sarah Buzby, Cindy Ledermann, Vicki Jaeger, Dana Koplik, Ann McNeill, Emily Kelly, Sharon Woloszyk, Julia Phelps, Tanya Mann, Rob Hudnut, David Wiebe, Tiffany J. Shuttleworth, Gabrielle Miles, Rainmaker Entertainment, Walter P. Martishius, Carla Alford, Rita Lichtwardt, and Kathy Berry

A GOLDEN BOOK • NEW YORK

BARBIE and associated trademarks and trade dress are owned by, and used under license from, Mattel, Inc.
Copyright © 2012 Mattel, Inc. All Rights Reserved.
www.barbie.com
Published in the United States by Golden Books, an imprint of Random House Children's Books, a division of Random House, Inc., 1745 Broadway, New York, NY 10019, and in Canada by Random House of Canada Limited, Toronto. No part of this book may be reproduced or copied in any form without permission from the copyright owner. Golden Books, A Golden Book, A Little Golden Book, the G colophon, and the distinctive gold spine are registered trademarks of Random House, Inc.
randomhouse.com/kids
Educators and librarians, for a variety of teaching tools, visit us at randomhouse.com/teachers
ISBN: 978-0-307-92979-2
Printed in the United States of America
10 9 8 7 6 5 4

Merliah Summers was excited. She was doing what she loved most—surfing! And after taming a monster wave, Merliah won the first round of the biggest surfing contest of the year. She was ahead of her rival, Kylie Morgan.

Merliah couldn't wait to tell her mom about winning the contest. After wishing on her magic necklace, the young surfer dove into the water. Merliah had a special secret—she was a mermaid princess! Her mother was Queen Calissa, ruler of the undersea kingdom of Oceana.

Calissa was very proud of her daughter for doing so well in the surfing contest. But the queen had news of her own to share. A special ceremony would soon be held in Oceana, during which Calissa would gain the power to make Merillia—the life force of the ocean.

Merliah could not take part in the ceremony. If she did, she would lose her ability to change into a human again. But the queen believed it was Merliah's duty as a princess to attend the ceremony.

Unfortunately, the Merillia ceremony was on the same day as the final round of Merliah's surfing competition. Merliah felt torn, but she told her mother that she would not be able to come. She didn't want to miss the contest.

Calissa was heartbroken.

After changing back into a human and returning to land, Merliah competed in the second round of the contest. This time, Kylie won. But Merliah received all the attention of the reporters and the fans because she had performed a daring handstand!

Kylie was wild with jealousy. She would have done anything to be in the spotlight.

By the ocean the next day, Kylie was astonished when a rainbow fish appeared in the waves and started talking to her. The fish's name was Alistair, and he told Kylie to steal Merliah's magic necklace. "You take the necklace, you take her powers," Alistair said.

Kylie obeyed and used Merliah's necklace to transform into a mermaid!

Alistair promised to take Kylie to someone who could teach her the secrets of surfing. Instead, the fish led her to a giant undersea whirlpool where Queen Calissa's wicked sister, Eris, was being held prisoner. Alistair pushed Kylie into the whirlpool, setting Eris free—and trapping Kylie at the bottom of the ocean!

Luckily, Snouts, Merliah's baby sea lion friend, had followed Kylie and Alistair. He heard Kylie's cries and hurried to the beach to alert Merliah.

On shore, Merliah was desperately searching for her missing necklace. Snouts got her attention. Realizing that something was wrong, Merliah quickly followed him.

Merliah couldn't change into a mermaid without her necklace, but she could still breathe underwater. Snouts led Merliah to the whirlpool. Together, they pulled Kylie out.

"The ocean is my life," Kylie told Merliah. "If your aunt is going to hurt it, I want to help stop her."

Meanwhile, ambassadors from the four corners of the ocean had gathered to help Queen Calissa with the Merillia ceremony. Each ambassador carefully placed a precious gem in a special location around the throne.

During the ceremony, magical midday light would reflect off each gem, giving the royal mermaid who sat on the throne the power to make Merillia.

As the attendees gathered, Eris appeared with her mean stargazer minions.

"Eris!" Calissa cried.

The evil mermaid cast a wicked spell that turned Calissa's tail to stone! The queen sank helplessly to the bottom of the ocean.

Eris cast spells on all the ambassadors one by one. She cackled gleefully as she sat on the throne. In a few moments, the midday sun would shine down, giving her the power to make Merillia—and rule the ocean!

Merliah and Kylie quickly came up with a bold plan. Using seaweed as harnesses, they lassoed Eris's stargazer fish and rode them like surfboards! While Merliah kept Eris busy, Kylie steered her stargazer straight into the evil mermaid—and knocked her off the throne!

Merliah climbed onto the throne, but the ceremony did not work because she was not a mermaid. Realizing what she had to do, Kylie took a deep breath and gave Merliah the magic necklace.

"I wish to become a mermaid!" Merliah said. Suddenly, she was bathed in the light of Merillia! The magic transformed Merliah into a beautiful mermaid with a long, gorgeous tail. She had completed the Merillia ceremony!

Eris tried to stop Merliah by casting a spell. But the Merillia reflected the spell right back at her! All her terrible spells were undone, and her worst nightmare came true—she grew legs and became human! "No!" Eris wailed. "It's impossible!"

In the meantime, Merliah rushed to place the magic necklace around Kylie's neck. "I wish to become a mermaid," Kylie whispered with her last breath—and turned back into a mermaid just in time.

With Eris's spell broken, Queen Calissa swam to the throne and hugged Merliah. "You'll find you can make Merillia doing anything you love," Calissa told her daughter.

Merliah was very happy—until she remembered that because she had taken part in the Merillia ceremony, she could never turn into a human again.

The next day, Merliah, Kylie, and Calissa swam up to the surface. As Kylie got ready to surf, Merliah said sadly, "I wish I had legs so I could show off my new surfing trick." To her surprise, she magically turned into a human!

"It must have been the ceremony!" Calissa told her daughter. "You can be a mermaid *or* a human!"

Merliah and Kylie surfed together in the final round of the competition. Kylie won, but Merliah couldn't have been happier. She had learned to make Merillia and saved Oceana—and gained a new friend and surfing buddy!